Jamaica and the Substitute Teacher

W9-BYG-281

Jamaica and the Substitute Teacher

Juanita Havill

Illustrated by Anne Sibley O'Brien

Houghton Mifflin Company

Boston

For Polly, Lorraine, Carol, Sheryl,
Elaine, Maxine, Audrey, Lisa, and Susan
—J. H.

For Sue Sherman,
from the beginning
—A. S. O'B.

Text copyright © 1999 by Juanita Havill
Illustrations copyright © 1999 by Anne Sibley O'Brien

All rights reserved. For information about permission
to reproduce selections from this book, write to
Permissions, Houghton Mifflin Company,
215 Park Avenue South, New York, New York 10003.

www.houghtonmifflinbooks.com

Library of Congress Cataloging-in-Publication Data

Havill, Juanita.
Jamaica and the substitute teacher / Juanita Havill ; illustrated by Anne Sibley O'Brien.
p. cm.
Summary: Jamaica copies from a friend during a spelling test because
she wants a perfect paper, but her substitute teacher Mrs. Duval helps
her understand that she does not have to be perfect to be special.
RNF ISBN 0-395-90503-6 PAP ISBN 0-618-15242-3
[1. Substitute Teachers—Fiction. 2. Teachers—Fiction. 3. Schools—Fiction. 4. Cheating—Fiction.
5. Self-esteem—Fiction.]
I. O'Brien, Anne Sibley, ill. II. Title.
PZ7.H1115Jaj 1999
[Fic]—dc21 98-29754 CIP AC

Manufactured in the United States of America
BVG 10 9 8 7 6 5 4 3

"Hurry, Brianna," Jamaica said. "I want to see who our substitute is."

Brianna caught up. "I hope she's nice."

"Me, too."

A woman wearing a silky blue and green dress and a blue scarf was writing on the blackboard. She turned around. "Good morning, students. My name is Mrs. Duval." She gave them name tags to fill out. "If you write your names on these, it will be easier for me to learn them. Did Mrs. Wirth tell you she'll be out of town all week?"

"She went to Ohio," Thomas said.

"Yes, she did. While she's gone, I plan for us to work hard, but we'll have fun, too." Mrs. Duval smiled at the class.

Jamaica gave a thumbs-up to Brianna.

"First, we're going to hunt for a hidden object. I hid it in the classroom before you came in." Mrs. Duval gave them two clues: "It's something that lives in Antarctica, and its name starts with the same letter as the object it is hidden in."

All the kids scrambled around the room, except Jamaica. Penguins! she thought. They had read about penguins last week.

She looked at the ledge by the window. She found a plastic penguin in one of the flowerpots.

"Very good, Jamaica. Tomorrow will be your turn to hide an object."

"I'll come early," said Jamaica.

Next they had reading groups.

"Nice job," Mrs. Duval said after Thomas read.

When Jamaica's turn came, she read loud and clear.
She knew all the words.

"You read very well," said Mrs. Duval.

Jamaica felt like singing.

In math class they did puzzles. Jamaica had all the right answers. So did Cynthia and Thomas. Mrs. Duval let them choose stickers to put on their packets. Jamaica chose a gray kitten with yellow eyes.

"Cats are my favorite animals," Jamaica told Mrs. Duval.

"I like cats, too," said Mrs. Duval.

After lunch Mrs. Duval read a story. Then it was time for spelling.

Oh no, Jamaica thought. She had forgotten about the test.

"Would you like a minute to look over the words?" Mrs. Duval asked.

"Yes," everyone said, except Thomas.

"I know all of the words already," he said.

I wish I did, Jamaica said to herself. She looked at the list and tried to memorize every word.

"Time to start," Mrs. Duval said.

The first five words were easy. Then Mrs. Duval said, "Calf."

Jamaica's mind went blank. She chewed on her pencil. She stared out the window. She closed her eyes. I'll never get a perfect paper, she thought. When she opened her eyes, she noticed Brianna's paper. She could see the letters, too. "C-a-l-f," Jamaica wrote on her paper.

Then she looked up.

Was Mrs. Duval staring at her? Jamaica looked back down at her paper. What would Mrs. Duval think if she had seen her copy?

"Okay, time to exchange papers," Mrs. Duval said, and she put the spelling list on the bulletin board.

Jamaica wrote "100%" on Brianna's paper. Brianna drew a happy face on Jamaica's and put "A++++" across the top.

When Jamaica got her test back, she crossed out the happy face. It's not a perfect paper even if it looks like one, she thought.

"Please pass your spelling papers to the front," Mrs. Duval said.

Jamaica put hers in her desk.

Next came art, Jamaica's favorite class, but she couldn't think of anything to draw.

"Jamaica, could you come here for a minute?"
Mrs. Duval said.

Jamaica got up and walked slowly to Mrs. Duval's
desk.

"Your spelling test isn't with the others, Jamaica.
Did you hand it in?"

Jamaica shook her head. "I can tell you my score."

"I'd like to see it," Mrs. Duval said.

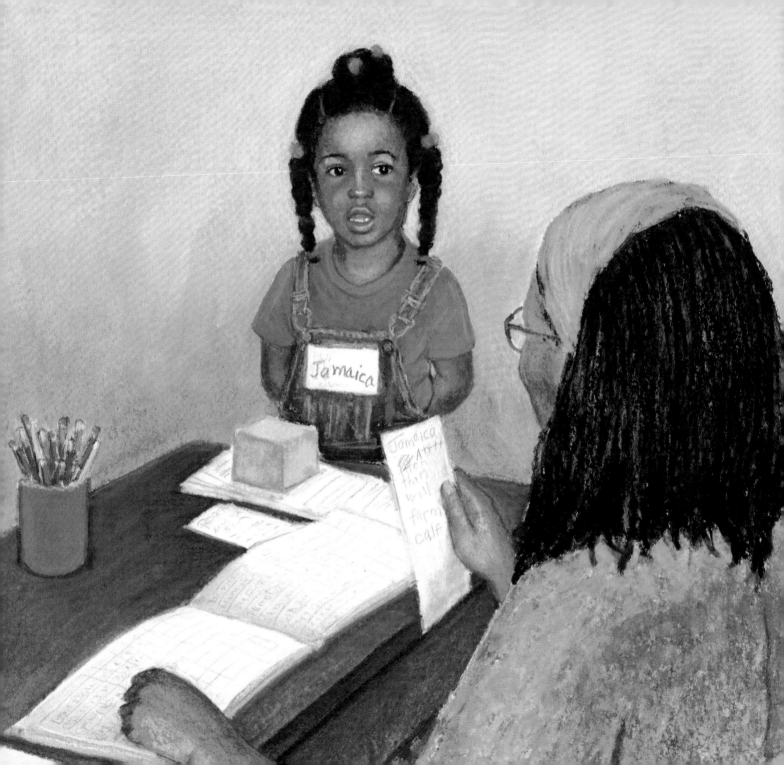

Jamaica showed her the paper. "It should say 'minus one.' I missed 'calf.'"

"'C-a-l-f' is right," Mrs. Duval said.

"But I didn't know how to spell it," said Jamaica. "I copied." Jamaica started to explain why she wanted to get a perfect paper, but it was too hard. "I'm sorry, Mrs. Duval," she said.

"I know," said Mrs. Duval. "It wasn't easy for you to tell me you copied." Mrs. Duval's voice was low, almost a whisper. "You know, Jamaica, you don't have to be perfect to be special in my class. All my students are special. I'm glad you're one of them."

"You are?" said Jamaica.

Mrs. Duval nodded.

"So am I," said Jamaica. "I hope you can be our substitute teacher again."

Jamaica sat back down at her desk and began to draw, but she didn't have time to finish her picture. She took it home and colored in the gray kitten and Mrs. Duval with her hundred braids. Then she wrote, "For Mrs. Duval from Jamaica." Tomorrow she would give her picture to Mrs. Duval. Tomorrow, first thing, she would hide an object in the classroom.

Jamaica couldn't wait.